As the Tide Came Flowing In

Sonya Taaffe

Nekyia Press

Boston

Published in the United States by Nekyia Press.

Additional copyright notices can be found on page 55.

Cover photo: Anna Tambour.

Cover design: Matthew Revert

https://www.matthewrevertdesign.com.

Interior design: Jeannelle M. Ferreira and Layla Lawlor.

ISBN: 978-0-578-97228-2

Library of Congress Control Number: 2021922702

Oh, we're bound for Mother Carey where she feeds her chicks at sea!

—Rudyard Kipling, "Anchor Song" (1893)

Contents

I. Ebb

Dive 3

The Coast Guard 4

The Parable of the Albatross 6

Firebrands 7

Capta 8

Colonial 9

He Should Marry the Daughter
of the Angel of Death 10

qe-ra-si-ja 11

Σειρήνοιϊν 13

The Secret Language of Water 15

II. Flood

As the Tide Came Flowing In 19

I

Ebb

Dive

Long after hours, when the sea-fog

coils in through the cigarettes

and the students are crying on each other's shoulders

like gulls,

the waitstaff in the glitter of glasses turn Neptune,

every bar becomes the belly of the whale.

Between one pour and the next,

lost ships sail back out of their bottles,

their cargo the only drink

that quiets the thirst of the drowned.

The plankton glimmers as the house lights dim.

The brass rail below the bar stools thrums slow ahead.

On nights like these, I drink absinthe

churned milky with sugar as the sea's green track

and watch Jonahs and sirens tangle

like trade winds, untwist like old rope,

but what do I know? No more than any other sailor

who drowned

looking for the mermaid at the bottom of their glass.

Sonya Taaffe

The Coast Guard

Winter had wrecked the ghost ship at our feet,

salt timbers heaved ashore on a rime of sand

our shadows froze to, pacing history—

storm-reef, sandspit, spermaceti, coal,

the hish and rattle of marram and beach plum

naked as pegged oak, so implicate with time

I wanted a ferryman for strand-flung souls

in the tarry seaweed heaps, a salt-stained

and steel-rimmed and cable-knit oracle

windward amid the haul and hail of voices,

tide-break and wrack and riving chains

outspoken, in the sunset waded thigh-deep

to take in his net the silver-sided drowning,

for those yet this side the water cry shoals,

a minister of grace and Neptune. We saw

a dog, two beachcombers, driftwood,

a camera-flash flurry of tourists over seals

like sleek piers and boulders, voyaging late.

Black against the dusk and amber, a paraglider

lifted wind-rocked from the dunes as we gazed,

unearthly as a petrel, the ship diminishing,

fire-gilt the coin of his passage over green.

5

The Parable of the Albatross

When I breathe, you can hear its restless feathers,

the great-winged wanderer of the sea-lanes

locked inside my ribcage

like a word inside a speckled shell.

The skim of the ice-white waves of the Southern Ocean

and the shearing rise of the wind over seal-black rocks

and the distance, the silence

made the language I speak first

before my throat closed with birdsong

and the red-breasted herald of northern spring.

The thickets are full of small wings and sweet voices,

the nests with delicate eggs, dapple-dyed.

Only the stranger who can match me dancing

and meet me balanced on the endless arc of air

will hear the deeper breath I take, unfolding

the full span of my ambition,

holding steady between the sea and the stars.

Firebrands

for Rob Noyes

With a face like a gallows woodcut

and a book of twenty-two names,

your hanging ancestor

looks at me out of Hawthorne,

the minister who steepled his hands at Salem

and died with blood in his throat.

History chokes up its emblems like affliction,

pins and witch-cakes,

chalices, pentacles, prayers.

We walked the wharves among tourists and museums,

shadows cracked into granite and sea air.

The demons I brought to our marriage

rustle like bats in the eaves,

read Kreytman and Margolin af yidish,

accept no one's fealty but their own.

Capta

I will not ask again if you prefer me

slumped in silver stamp of date palm's shadow,

Rome at my back, my grief bowed to its chains.

The broken sibyl mourns her shattered laws,

her children fighting doomed and rag-shod

or dissolving, quick as candles, to the wind of history.

You like my face in that half-blistered filmstrip,

that canceled passport, that marble weathered gold.

I will not ask—I know—you never saw me

standing beneath the emperor's brother's triumph

whose pride, bold in lost bronze, mine outlived.

I walked dry bricks of baths and theaters, singing

that jargon of poets and partisans, desert

diaspora. Here I still am, no memorial.

I live on the other riverbank.

I take the trains.

Colonial

How can I picture you, ghost from a colder diaspora,

farther from me than Carthage or Vishnevets?

How can I acknowledge your things of whiteness

mine? Born too late for never-setting empires,

the backwash of your blood-tide

lapped me in the atlas of the New Jerusalem

where in the secretary hand of monsters at the margins

cultivation was rendered wilderness

and the Devil was a black man with a book.

I descend more easily by Avernus

than I can follow you up that shining city's hill,

shadowing your name that almost ran down to me.

We with wild geese and pogroms in our families

carry the homes we know we must always leave.

No one who brings an empire everywhere with him,

my Puritan haunting, gets out of it alive.

He Should Marry the Daughter
of the Angel of Death

for Lila Garrott

Come, my beloved, still so shy,

so many husbands consigned to your embrace

like onions headfirst to the ground,

no wonder you wrapped yourself in your father's

    forgetfulness

and fled the world, hunting for the bitter drop.

Lead me out, the groom among the gravestones

that crowd this blackest of weddings

like beggars to the dance.

The demon-king himself would have raised you temples,

but mine was the mouth you drank from, a cup of pearls.

Let the names we buried keep your father looking

too late to bless us

beneath the canopy of his suffocating wings.

qe-ra-si-ja

From Piraeus, we could have flown to Santorini,

but we had made our plans for Thera

on a boat of banked oars and far-faring eyes.

Dolphins no bluer than the water

wreathed our wake,

the nearing seawalls whitened

with the slap of salt, not ash.

With words from Phaistos or Arkalochori,

the captain offered us sweet, dark, tiny figs.

You will learn the weaving of eel-baskets,

swim with the sponge divers and haul out

shaking water thick as bronze from your seal's hair.

I will learn the singing of tales,

not their stealing,

and write nothing Alice Kober could not crack.

We watched the contrails over the caldera ring,

white as pumice and four thousand years younger.

Sonya Taaffe

Under the sea-charting stars, the work

always needs doing, gathering saffron, stories,

sea daffodils despite the fire.

Σειρήνοιϊν

Here to this island of flowers and bones,

not many come

but my song draws them

like the riptide a drowning sailor

or the noose a broken heart.

The great ships founder, break their treasure at my feet—

oxhides of copper, black-figured wine-bowls,

amphorae smashed hollow as the chests of their crew.

The fishermen's nets

drift slack-jawed in the tide,

the wind strings a lyre of their empty throats.

Soldiers have left their shields and greaves,

poets their salt-dried laurels

and all their long bones to the sun.

I tell lies to no one.

I pledge what I give.

The truth is the breaker of men.

But come of your own soul's singing,

beyond the shoals' wreck and stagger

and the billows of asphodel,

with your grief-hacked hair

and the ashes you loved in your arms

and I will give you the choice of heroes

who must outlive the war:

on the dark earth and beneath it,

my art is memory.

Demeter's daughter passed this pomegranate to me,

Syrinx's mother entrusted me with these pipes.

Take the fruit from my hand

and I will grant you its wet red forgetfulness,

the sleep of a seed in the rind of the unasking earth.

Take the song from my mouth,

take the stormwind from within you,

and I will tell the truth with you.

The Secret Language of Water

How could you not hear it,

secret as tears

or a storm coming on across sea,

the trickling whisper of steerage and black coral,

sunken constellations, packet liners, trawlers

and chains?

Who could find you the rope to bind

your heartache, the wax to close your ears

to their own blood?

Out on the waves we might watch them for miles,

the drowned and the moonstruck

in the gyre of history,

dreaming their shoreward roads

with maps wet as handkerchiefs.

How could we not wring them out

to read them,

their long record of losses and horizons

the lagan of our hearts, the buoy calling us back?

NecronomiCon Providence 2019

II

Flood

As the Tide Came Flowing In

She died in springtime, out of sight of the sea. So young, her family said, such a terrible loss, and so soon after her husband's tragedy. But then she had never been strong and she had married so poorly, throwing away her youth and her prospects on a sailor man who kissed his wife twice and left her for years to the desolate company of the cold Atlantic shore and the foreign trinkets he sent home, as if Chinese lacquer and Polynesian boar's teeth could replace the solace of decent society or the warmth of a child. Small wonder if she had sunk into fancies and loneliness, watching her life drift away from her like trash on the tide, smaller wonder still if she had yielded at last to the persuasions of a man no more scrupulous than her tide-tossed husband, if closer to hand—but the dead were sinless, she was dead now and her bastard with her, and the Bridgmans of Boston wore black gloves and jet pins for their wayward daughter and said very little at the service. The youngest grandson squalled in the arms of his mother, his father the sober young banker cleared his throat above his stiff collar. In the Public Garden, the willows were yellowing like old paper and the bronzes of Washington and

Sumner were tarnished with mist in the morning; the slates and granite slabs of the North Burying Ground were cold as weeping to touch. The family plot was conspicuous by the absence of her name. Perhaps there were limits to the sinlessness of the dead after all.

She was an old woman in springtime, or a woman who would have been old if she had lived to measure her life by experience rather than existence, nearly sixty years behind her eyes and more than thirty of them within the tall red bricks of Danvers State. By then there was no shortage of shaking, screaming, sleepless people, but most of them were hiding from mortar-shells, not seashells; the waves that engulfed their dreams were of shattered horses and mud-toppling men, not the Atlantic's mare-grey breakers or the Pacific's vast blue swell. They covered their eyes against blown-off faces, not weed-picked hair or sea-lichen scaled over a smile. But they would not speak much of the war to her, the nurses who combed her hair and brought her books and pinned her wrists when she still struggled after so many years, gasping with the breathless cold inside her; it was not news that would soothe a troubled woman to hear. *Our brave boys are fighting for us,* they told her, and she could not stop thinking of her own brave boy in a trench of sea-ice, glass-bubbled pale and impervious to the pounding of fists. When they left her to gaze out through the high windows that overlooked the green embroidery of the gardens and the patients who tended their elegant designs, she whispered, *I am fighting, too,* though she was no longer sure for what. Silence, perhaps, or simply solitude. Eight miles inland, she was never without the sea.

~~~

Her husband came home in summer, calling so softly under her window that at first she thought she dreamed him, his voice as natural in the night as the mewing of gulls or the heart's rush of the tide. *Elizabeth, Lizzie-o, my darling, Lizzie . . .* She had grown used to those dreams; they sharpened as each second summer stretched interminably toward autumn and the *Galatea's* return, the pitiless clock of the Arctic fishery that kept her husband landlocked above the sun all winter while she mended shirts and thawed driftwood for the fire and diced the potatoes and the salt pork finer and finer, counting the days toward the opening of the ice. She had kissed him last on the docks of New Bedford when the winds were still fickle with April of '84; now it was June again, when she picked serviceberries from their windbent bushes and shelled sweet peas with her feet bare in the sandy earth, and she had been a whaleman's wife long enough to know the difference between the skin-hunger of a dream and the sound of her name in the cricket-warm night, the sea breeze
~~~

rustling the tall grasses down on the dunes. Quick and caressing, a laugh in his voice with no one to wake but his wife—*Lizzie, can you hear me? Oh, come down, Lizzie-o, come down.* His mother's shawl was ghosting the back of the chair before her dressing table, its lace floating white as a gannet's wing. Elizabeth McKay took a candle, a deep breath, and went downstairs to let her husband in.

For a moment in the colorless wash of the moon, she thought she was still dreaming. His face was a figurehead's, smiling through salt ruin; she saw the flowering fire of anemones on his shoulders, a starfish stretched like a hand laid to his breast. She smelled the deep salt thunder of the sea. Then her hand trembled, slewing his shadow across the threshold and the little sprigs of dry wild rose and violets pinned for luck at the door, and in the candlelight she saw him as real and as dear as their wedding day: her Ezra, still the bright-earringed boy with his crooked grin and his hair that tousled like barley, his eyes as blue as new paint on a carousel. His peacoat was shabby with salt at the cuffs and elbows, his shirt as stained as an old map. His fingers sliding under the night-loosened braid of her hair smelled of tar and coal soap, faintly the grease of smoke that every whaleship stank of, deep-dyed into sails and decking and men's skins. She turned her face to his palm and breathed him in.

"Oh, Lizzie."

He had never had many fine endearments for her, only the soft, wondering turn of her name in his mouth, as if each time it amazed him to find her still waiting, to find *her*. Courting, he had been brash, turning new treasures out of his pockets with each call: blush-colored conch pearls and stubs of palm-pink coral, sharks' teeth, star knots, a barbed fish hook carved from tortoiseshell winking cat's-eye in his hand as he offered it to her. A little wooden walrus, such as he said he had seen the Nunatsiarmiut hunting in the summer months along the shores of Baffin Island. A jagging wheel of whale ivory, though she was a competent piemaker at best. He was a boatsteerer with a seventy-fifth of the profits to his name each voyage and her father was a Boston businessman with three daughters, the youngest alone mad enough to entertain the attentions of a chance-met sea-talker, a well-spoken harpooneer with ambitions of ship's master. He brought her a pair of brass knuckles and showed her how to weight her fist with them, a pocket sextant and taught her to steer by the stars. *When I have my own ship, you'll come with me, Lizzie, you'll see. And none of those lady ships where a master's wife has nothing to do but make soft conversation and read the Bible to green hands—I'll have you for navigator. You've the steadiest eye I know,* and she heard again the Irish in his voice like a flash of fish-silver, his American-born coffin ship's legacy.

Elizabeth had waited one voyage for him, for letters from ports more remote than even her tea-trading grandfathers had spied; by the spring of '79 she had known she would not wait another. They were married in a seamen's chapel, shy and breathless, where not even her parents' hard silence echoing down from Dorchester like a winter front could dim how fiercely she felt herself smiling. Her husband held her as if a storm would take her from his arms, all his body seal-hot against hers as she gripped him in the same starving wonder. Two days later, he sailed for the Horn.

"Hello, Ezra," she said now, quite calmly. He was watching her as steadily as she remembered, his gaze roving unashamed from her hairline to the undone buttons of her nightshirt, her hand on the door and the candle paling upward in the other like a fairy tale reversed—Psyche wakened, her winged husband unmasking himself and all the tragedy over before it began. She stepped back, just enough to show him the darkened house beyond. "Will you come in?"

She had been jealous once of the women in other ports, the men who came ashore to them; she had held herself up against Inuit women with ocean-black hair and all else pale as spermaceti, Hawaiian women as strong in the water as sun-backed dolphins, and herself a graceless stick of a girl with hair as sandy as East Beach and an indifferent freckled skin, the despair of her mother's bronze taffetas and rosy silks. She could not run rigging or carve a whale's tooth. She swam better than her husband, with his sailor's superstitious unease in the sea itself, but the knots she tied were string around brown paper, not heavy rope around bollards and bitts; her fingers had been slow to learn kitchen knives and copper pans, accustomed to deckle-edged pages, embroidery needles, piano keys. She would never heave an iron into a whale's hide. But Ezra talked only of the day when she would go to sea with him, not the hindrance she must be aboard ship, of the countries he would show her and the acquaintances he would introduce her to, not their better claims on him, and when he dropped his boots at the foot of the bed and pulled her down beside him, he did not touch her like something fragile or dutiful or rare but as if the knowledge of her body, along with stars, spouts, and card-sharping, were something he carried for everyday employment. *You haven't forgotten me,* she said after the second voyage, and Ezra actually laughed, so unreservedly that he cracked the top of his skull against the headboard and had to curl into her arms, wincing, instead of kissing her. *The way a man forgets his blood, Lizzie-o,* and then it was kisses again and heat and salt and his fingers combing dreamily through her hair afterward until it shone across the bedclothes beneath them, rayed out like a lionfish's spines. After that she envied his crewmates, but it was not such a clawing, self-sick thing. *You can tell the islands a long way off from the clouds that gather over them, like pillars of white jade. Once you've seen them with the sunset underneath, all afire, redder than you'd believe . . . You should see the size of the moon over the sea.* Utterly confident that someday she would, only a matter of skill and savings: *And we'll never go near Southwest Jimmy's again, that stinking crimp. Or his shite beer.*

And he had done well for a whaleman, she knew that living in her small, slant-eaved house with a view of Clarks Cove. Instead of a rented room on Union Street and a shared parlor smelling of other men's hair oil and other women's perfume, she had the whole windswept horizon to come down to in the mornings; if she lived like a hermit without gaslight or Edison's electricity, she had not set herself alight with kerosene or whale oil yet. She had china plates on her mantel and whorled shells the same peach-yellow as a September sunset beside them and twice a week she walked to the markets of Cheapside like any housewife with an icebox to fill. She had a four-poster bed with clean-boiled sheets on it and it was not always empty, not every other fall when the *Galatea*'s fourth boatsteerer came home. Upstairs in the shifting light of the small, thick-leaded windows and flat-wick lamps, they relearned each other: scars, smiles, weight and work, stories in the skin. Ezra was not the only one carrying time like the tattoo at his wrist, gunpowder-blue under tan. Once she had reached to touch the sliced-red snarl still fading under his hair—a bottle-smashing brawl on Kekerten Island, overwintering in '81—and forgot until he exclaimed over it the long, pale weal twisting up her forearm where a cart full of empty oil casks had knocked her down on North Water Street.

Penelope waited ten years, she said simply, the year the ice was bad in the Davis Strait and the whaling worse, the men sour-tempered and the ship a creaking, smoke-ragged hulk by the time she limped into warmer waters, the year Ezra signed on to a Brava packet after two days at home—six weeks across the North Atlantic at the cusp of winter—just to hand her his advance. *How should I complain of three?*

From the other side of the pillow, Ezra said, "Did you get my letters?"

This time she was watching the lines around his eyes, the faint wheat-gold bristle along his jaw in the lamplight. "Two posted from Talcahuano," Elizabeth said. The names ran in her head like a song, cold places and hot, roaring cities and shantytowns. "One from Frisco and three from Honolulu. One from Sitka."

"I wrote you another from Point Barrow."

"You beat it home."

His earring winked at her, a plain gold spark. "I couldn't wait. Not for you."

The quilt half tangled around them was new last winter, striped calico diamonds and six-pointed stars the color of milky porridge; the air was warm enough to draw sweat where their bodies touched and Elizabeth shifted deeper into its weight, tucking her chin down into a fold as if she were chilled. Something she had said was wrong as a slack string in a piano, a quarter-tone off-key. "But the *Galatea—*"

"Oh, Lizzie, Lizzie-o. I'd come back from Hilo for you. I'd come back from Hell."

He said it as lightly and as fervently as any other love-words he had ever spoken to her and she was colder, staring at him. The letters from Honolulu had come wrapped and waxed in oil-paper, enclosing a springy rib of whalebone etched with two different type of whale, the bull-headed sperm and the bowhead with its underslung smile. *Vieira says it is as good a likeness as you will find until you see one for yourself in its native water. There was a sunset last night like a parrot's feathers and I hoped there was a sun rising like it in New Bedford. He must greet you for me when he sees you first.* He had always written more laboriously than he spoke, in a spiky, scratchy hand that lost ink around the margins of the page in little sprays and constellations; she wrote back in her slanting copperplate and sometimes their letters met. So many gone astray in gales, misunderstandings, overworked clerks' offices, crossing without making landfall. It was not the right worry; she could not put the right words around it. She heard herself say, small and dully, "Because I am safe."

"Oh, Lizzie." The featherbed humped and shifted under them as Ezra turned on his side, put his chin on his fist to look at her for so long that she began to feel like a stranger, equivocal as she had not been since the first years of their marriage when she watched the waves run white against the rocks of Clarks Point and could not imagine what they would say to one another when her whaleman returned. His mouth creased a little, not enough for mockery, unless he meant it for himself. "Elizabeth. You're not *safe.*"

He was warm everywhere, his breath quick on her skin and his scent as sharp and familiar as the wind off the sea; he was sunburnt and blue-eyed and beloved, with more to say to her than they had always had time for. He was as much a stranger as every time he came home and she laughed as suddenly as she had felt desolate the moment before, feeling his fair hair sun-shot with silver frisking in the hollow of her shoulder, before he rolled her over in the sheets that smelled of salt air and sweet lavender and she took hold of him, took him in, drew him under. Breathless at the crisis, he said, "I do love you, Elizabeth." It was the last clear thing she heard. The sky beyond the curtains was banding the pearl-blue of the inside of a mussel shell, the stars going out in the clouds before dawn. Her husband's arms were fast around her and she fell into sleep like a clear black current, a bright cameo of their bedroom receding above her like a rippling lens of sky.

She surfaced without dreaming into the noise of gulls, clamoring a bedlam of grey and white feathers beyond her window as keenly as around the casks at Merrill's Wharf; there was as strong a sea-smell in the air. The quilt was too heavy and she pushed it off before thinking of Ezra who might have been dreaming of frozen rigging and cliffs of snow like whale's teeth; of the ice beginning to close as the brief Arctic summer ended, the sun dipping beneath the low wet earth again. She was tallying autumn's responsibilities in her head before she remembered. Downstairs in the kitchen were broad beans and small new strawberries, upstairs was a stickiness of heat and more windows that needed opening. She knew then what the right worry would have been.

Even then she was not afraid, only a little disenchanted— some with the dream, more with herself, scraping love together from wishful sleep and sea air. Wry-smiling, her hair loose to her waist, Elizabeth McKay sat up in bed to pull her empty blankets straight, and then she saw what lay beside her on the pillow, strewn through the sheets like storm-wrack in the unmistakable morning light, and then she began to scream.

~~~

The child came in winter, the last blustery days when even the salt cod were powdery at the bottom of their barrel and the sea smashed itself against the shore as if to scour it clean, but she had ceased to mark the seasons months ago. The east wing was for women and between the grey slates of its roof and the white plaster of its walls very little changed except for the pallor of the light and the snow thickening the panes. She hung in the light like a swelling drop of water, drawn by gravity to bulge and break, like a moon so low in the sky that it raked the jealous tides behind it. She screamed in the nurses' arms and watched her own blood running over hospital sheets and chafing hands. It would not find its way down to the sea here, drawn off by the pine-matted earth like a balked and buried stream; she could not follow it down to her love.

Over and over, they told her her husband was dead, as if she had not heard the first time when she was nearly six months pregnant with her quickening son. The *Galatea* had brought the news in October when she returned from the Arctic grounds and
~~~

the cooper who bunked above Ezra could tell the story, there in the cloud-scudded sunlight on Central Wharf with Elizabeth gripping his hands as though the birth-pangs twisted through her already. But it was something else, coring as disbelief as the men came tramping down the scrubbed gangplank with their kit bags over their shoulders and her Ezra was nowhere among them, not his harvest hair, not his salt-stained jacket, not his candlelit grin. All summer she had haunted the shore, praying for her courses, scrubbing the floor with sand; she burned the curtains and the bedclothes one night on the dry granite blocks of the seawall, watching the reflections break on the scale-black water like a beacon light, and still rose each morning with their harbor-smell in her head. As her belly rounded, she went less and less often into town, clutching shawls about her shoulders when she had to, pushing her way through the crowds on Pleasant Street as if she recognized no one among them, willing even the kindest questions away: she had no answers anymore. Her dreams were full of monstrous things, half-transparent skin stretched over half-luminous bones, cold blood in colder dark. For once she was grateful for her parents' disdain; she could not imagine telling them of their grandchild.

I am sorry, Mrs. McKay. I sent his letter from Frisco, soon as we were coming home, the letter that had never reached her, the letter that Ezra had not sent before he drowned. On the docks of New Bedford, she heard from a stranger what she should have known from a dream: how the whaleboats had gone out on the ice-lashed waves off Point Barrow, the new summer sun glinting thin as isinglass on the blue-scattered dip and fall of the Beaufort Sea, and the stout bowhead had blown twice as if hailing the whalers, who laughed. They were not noisy; they drew the boat alongside the rolling, slate-shining bulk of whale, and Ezra McKay had readied his iron, as neat and handy a man as ever shed blood to the sea—but when the harpoon went home and the powder went off, instead of dying or sounding for a sleigh-ride the whale heaved itself over in the freezing water as if it knew exactly where its tormentors lay. The iron-black flukes raised high, smashed down. Five men were pulled from the blood-strung wreckage of the whaleboat, but the boatsteerer never came back up. The more romantic or morbid among the *Galatea*'s crew imagined him tangled in the line's coils, pulled into the abyss after his own iron, as if the whale had turned fisher for him; Abraão Vieira, less sentimentally inclined and with an eye to the floes crushing close around the *Galatea*'s hull, spoke only of a man's chances between the ice of the pack and the breath-snatching sea. *We looked for him, Mrs. McKay. I swear we don't leave while he had one damn chance.* Around them the traffic of strangers bobbed and butted like brash ice, though she was the one insensible as a frozen thing. *Mr. Vieira, I believe you. Your kindness—I can't say—* He was not pulling away from her, haggard as she must have looked with blue-milk shadows under her eyes and her beach-colored hair pinned badly, fraying and flagging in the raw bright kick of the wind; his eyes were green as shallows, his crisp hair fairer than the long hands steady around her own, and she knew him from Ezra's letters, Vieira who knew something about every creature they might see on their voyage. He had slept more nights within the sound of her husband's breathing than she had herself. He was not lying to her. Elizabeth wanted to weep on his shoulder, this Creole man from Cape Verde in his faded red shirt and his old brown coat; steel-straight as a daughter of Thomas Bridgman, she let go his hands and said in the voice of her mother's drawing room, *I am in your debt, Mr. Vieira. To receive dreadful news from a friend is to know at least that the shock is not singularly borne.* The hard gulp of breath that finished the sentence was not grief. Her dead man's child kicked her a second time beneath the ribs and she must have said something to the living man to take her leave of him, but all she could remember afterward was the taste of tarnished pennies in her mouth, the whirl of cracked-china sky, and the cobbles pitching up at her as sickeningly as waves through a stove boat before Vieira caught her as no one had her husband, belly-up like a storm-heeled ship, a landed whale.

She would never know if it was the young doctor summoned from his practice on William Street who betrayed her, his raw-freckled face eclipsing Vieira's like an anxious and self-important moon. She was sure only that it could not have been Vieira himself, whose short scrawled letters the attendants handed on to her as if it were an ordinary thing for a madwoman to read her own mail. Sometimes in the late months of her confinement she dreamed of him, carving a cradle from wood as white as whalebone; the shavings drifted around him like snow or the feathers of far northern birds and he smiled over his work, the scrape and tap of his chisel an icy tattoo. Sometimes she dreamed of Ezra, real dreams that left nothing of themselves in the morning but the aching gulf of grief and the slow grinding beneath that of something she could not name so easily, deeper than mere fear. She did not dream of her father railing his invocations of whoredom and disease, her mother weeping as softly as a knife. Over and over, she repeated as calmly and clearly as she knew how that she carried no one's child but her husband's, which only another lunatic would have believed.

Had she been correctly insane like her wardmates with their starvations and compulsions, their manias and melancholias, Elizabeth thought she would have taken great comfort in the Danvers Lunatic Hospital with its wrought iron roof-crowns and its granite stairs, the flowering beds of its gardens and the sturdy fields of its farm. It was airy and industrious, sometimes obtuse but rarely cruel; she had smiled to see the profusion of dahlias inside and out of Dr. Kirkbride's model asylum. It was not his fault that she raked at the well-turned earth with her nails when offered a hand in the apple harvest, as if she might scratch down to some sunken vein of sea, that she could not handle the rushes of basket-weaving without thinking of slippery kelp and knotted wrack, the seaweed she had never seen tangled about her love's head. Given a wooden puzzle, she made a long skeleton of its pieces and imagined the whale itself, like a spirit flame rising. Everywhere were things growing, things rooted, things dying back to black earth under flying snow. She could not lie easy, so far inland that her husband could not find her. Sometimes she plotted what the staff called an *elopement*, disappearing over the dry stone wall where the trains whistled past Asylum Station. Even Salem would have been close enough to breathe of the sea.

Instead she tasted the salt of her own bitten lips and the carbolic sting of sweat, her body itself the wounded, ungovernable, thrashing leviathan; she dragged breath after breath of choking thin air and screamed for Ezra until the doctor's terse orders and the sweetness of ether muffled her away. Far and blurred as the dim end of a telescope, her husband sat at the foot of the bed, casting lots with dice of red coral on the starch-white sheets. The cradle rocked beside him, whiter still in shadows of glacier-blue and aurora-green. She could not ask him if the drowned felt so curiously peaceful, tugged and buoyed by pressures so vast and distant as to feel like natural movement; she could not even see him anymore, only the rush of bubbles, silver and glass-bottle green. The dice fell through her fingers into the dark. When the world drained back in, something small and white-swaddled was being placed in her arms, a doll arranged with a smaller doll to hold. "A fine strong boy, Mrs. McKay," she heard echoing from one of the nurses' mouths, genuine warmth that she could not quite feel through her numbed and swollen flesh; her stomach rolled as though she had been too long at sea and put suddenly ashore. The calm white walls gleamed around her like close-packed snow. "Wouldn't you like to hold your beautiful boy?"

It seemed to take a hundred years to close her eyes and open them, to understand what she was being offered and what she possessed. She had never coveted children as her sisters did, though she had said all the right things over the pink-and-white faces of their infants and their dark or fair downs of hair as they drowsed or mewed in their nursemaids' arms; it had frightened her to want one from her whaleman and then frightened her more to think of some fault in herself, five fruitless years on. For all she knew, her husband's children were scattered across the coasts of three oceans, never to be known to her, or perhaps even to him. She had never been sure what it would mean to ask. The bed was hospital-cornered and empty again, but she could still see the dice falling, blood-bright with pips of bone. "Yes," Elizabeth said. Her throat felt thick as drunkenness; she tried to clear it. She could name this one for his father. "Yes, I would," and she looked down through the frozen fog of ether into her child's face for the first and last time.

She was told afterward, during the first use of mechanical restraint, that she had tried to kill her child, to wring its neck between her hands as though she broke a lobster's back. She could not make them understand that what had slid out between her thighs on a breaking wave of blood was no more her child than the mess of shells and mud and seaweeds reeking by daylight in her bed had been her husband nine months before. Her son was lost fathoms below the Arctic ice with his father—only a truly mad woman would have mistaken the sea's leavings for anything else. She had seen the red grease of its skin like stripped blubber, heard it shriek like a mobbing seabird as it was snatched from her arms. Its eyes were a glaucous blank of waters, its mouth as mindlessly gaping as gills. Even its smell was murky as low tide under the sterile washes of green soap and bichloride. How could she ever have fretted that the sea was too far to find her? Her own body's salt was its signature. How had she been fool enough to fancy it her ally? It brought back nothing it had not already disdained to keep. For the sake of one short summer night, she had let it in and now she would never get free of its hollow roar in her ears, its restless beat in the slim veins of her wrists; she tried. Stronger hands than her own wrestled her down against cool cast iron that rang like nacre with her screaming, wrapped her fast in wet white sheets like a burial at sea. She had ceased to dream of Ezra with or without cuttlefish's ink running down his face like tears, of Vieira in his well-worn leather apron casting a weather eye over clouds as pale and solid as the sunlit beach of stones, of her parents whose final visit had made her laugh, raucous and stabbing as a gull, with their useless horrorstricken courtesies. *Take him,* she had jeered, no model patient with her insomniac bruises and her ward in the outermost wing, her grin like a moray's jaws, *take him for all the good it will do you. His father'll come for him in the end.* She did not dream once of the child, abyssal or adopted. She dreamed of cowries and ivory, pancake ice and palm wine, sealskins, skuas, the great moon over the sea.

By then she had lost her parole of the grounds, for glimpsing the Atlantic from Hathorne Hill: they still thought she screamed in terror or insanity. Alone with her books and cut flowers and the writing paper for which she was sometimes permitted a pen, Elizabeth thought that even a maelstrom could not rage as she did, a tsunami, a typhoon. Even the last resort of chloral could not drown her too deep for the tide.

~~~

Her husband came back in autumn, when the rain dripped off the slates and gables and the leaf-stripped trees bent like seagrass in the wind, while far and farther off the guns stormed at Amiens and Megiddo and Meuse-Argonne and she did not hear them, though she could have stood at the height of the Himalayas and not been out of earshot of the sea. Some years she thought it grew louder as the summer waned and the Arctic season with it; then she remembered how many years it had been. She did not know if men went out any longer in ships out of New Bedford or San Francisco to hunt the whale at one cold end of the world or another; if their women still waited for them as Ezra had sworn that as a captain's wife she would not have to do. Perhaps there were neither whales nor women left anymore, only men at war on
~~~

a cold, bristling ocean of sunken liners and tin fish. She had no one to ask; even the new admissions were more likely to tell stories of ferry crossings or childhood holidays and she had heard the doctor warning the younger nurses not to encourage her during her nervous times. She watched the haymaking from her windows, the harvesting of squash and corn and turnips, the healthful markers of the farming year. On very good days, she read quietly in the women's pavilion, her still thickly braided hair a beach of grey sand. She was not supposed to describe herself so, as she was not supposed to say that the clouds above the burnt treeline were white whales' bellies, the late September sky they shoaled in the hungry, reflecting blue of the water she did not need to see.

She had no other words for the moon when it fell in watery vanes through the glass beyond the window guards and mottled the floor like foam. The room's small furnishings might have been hummocks of ice or heaps of whales' bones, without motion or color, all but the man in the dark coat turning back from the night view of the well-gardened grounds. He stood in the moonlight as though in a backwash of waves, his shadow dripping from his sea-boots; his hair still fell in the same fair untidy sheaf, but it was mossy with algae and a snail moved slowly across his cheek, browsing like a beauty mark among the barnacles and small wrack. "Oh, Lizzie," she heard: something in his voice hissed and swallowed, the dog whelk's rasp against black crusts of mussels, the suck of the tide at rocks and pilings and human feet planted in sliding sand. His coat was ragged as shipwreck, or perhaps it was partly changed to weed. When he held his hand out to her, it was full of pale ambergris. "Oh, Lizzie, my Lizzie-o."

Cold in her madwoman's bed, Elizabeth knew it for a dream. Ezra McKay would never have appeared to her in this drowned half-shape, her whaleman who had loved her enough to come back from the gates of death and the grip of the back-breaking sea to lie all night in her arms until the daylight melted him like a fairy tale, forgetting in the inhuman roll of the tide how much it would twist her to lose him again, how easily the sea could steal through his longing into hers, worse than any indecent disease. Only the gold in his ear gleamed true and imperishable. The rest was echo, water-warped and mocking. "Ezra," she whispered finally, because it was the wet shadow of her husband's face looking back at her with those comber-pale eyes, the tattoo at his wrist prickling with olivine spines. His fingernails looked like stone. She was not a sane woman; she had no need of politeness, even when her voice shook. "What are you doing here?"

He took another step closer; his shadow pooled along the floorboards like polished ink. That voice she could not recognize sounded as if it were choking on sandy water, on heart-stopping ice: "I couldn't wait."

There was a great wave rising in her throat; she swallowed it before it could wake the night nurse or one of her neighbors and recognized it as rage from the way it hurt, as familiar as the waterlogged phrases across thirty-three years. She imagined her husband falling bonelessly from blue waters into black, his life's store of words like stones in his pockets for the sea to tumble and cast ashore, none of them meaning any longer what they had gone down saying. The parrot's feathers. The white jade clouds. Her name. She could not pray to a God she had long ago ceased to credit, but she thought suddenly of distant Sundays: *and there was no more sea.* In her old woman's dry night voice, "Damn you to Hilo *and* Hell," Elizabeth said to the sea on the other side of her husband's face, and struggling out of bed reached for the wall switch to dispel its specter once and for all.

In the soft bloom of gaslight, Ezra McKay looked not a day older than his drowning. His coat was weather-worn melton cloth neatly mended at the seams, his wind-creased face scrubbed clean; he looked at the ambergris in his hand as if he had forgotten the time and put it back in his pocket, out of which small crabs did not scuttle. No salt water ran from his sleeve as he reached to pull the cane-back rocker over to the bedside, though it crackled beneath his weight as he took a seat in it, leaning a little forward as he had always, eagerly done. His hair shone strand by strand like a harvest field. As if it mattered very little, Elizabeth saw that he cast no shadow except across himself, and the rest of the ward in their paralyses and psychoses and plain heartaches slept around them, and she did not know anymore if she had turned up the light, if she was dead or dreaming or he was, if the sea, unbelievably, had not cheated her after all. She did not know anything except that she had heard of ghosts with consciences, but she had so rarely seen Ezra with one, she was not inclined to believe she had invented the look of it on him, stranger than the shape-changing of death.

To her husband this time, Elizabeth McKay said, "I didn't get your letter."

"I sent none."

"You must have known where to find me."

His brows winced together; she saw the reddened fleck of a cut through one, so fresh she knew it had not quite healed when he died. "I never meant to leave you so, Lizzie. Eighteen months to the Arctic grounds and back, that was all."

His living face was sober, but his voice was still the waves' wet growl, easy to be angry with. She was bitterly conscious of her spotted hands, her sagging wrists, her parchment throat. "And yet you left me waiting twenty times that."

"I am sorry, Lizzie. I am sorry. Sorry as I can be." He had the red and white dice in his hands again, turning and clicking like loose shingle in the tide; Elizabeth wondered if they had come from some port of his last voyage or some gambling hell undersea. Perhaps he had traded with one of his shipmates for them. She would not ask if Vieira was dead. A little wryly, Ezra added, "There's no ship's chronometer," and that was another question she had to close her mouth on. He was no table-rapper's guide, even if she could picture him far more readily on the decks of a ghostly whaler than reposing among some airy haven of harps.

"Then what brought you back to port at last?"

She said it like a challenge; she saw him hear it as one, a slight, tightening wave across his face that looked mostly surprised, as she imagined it must have looked even in the midst of brawls and brothels, ever the blue-eyed innocent with blood in his hair. Or it was real surprise, because he was saying as carefully as he could with his throat of thick waters, "The tide turned, Lizzie. The heart's tide. You."

In her early years at Danvers, she had written more letters than she could count, long, rambling, sometimes ink-blotted and more often furiously steady outpourings of everything she expressed otherwise in the howls of her voice and the wrenchings of her body, all the words sane women were not supposed to know. Sometimes she had rolled them into bottles of thick-molded amber glass whose corks still smelled of medicines, sometimes folded them with great care into the small envelopes provided through the good offices of the State Board of Lunacy and Charity; she had given all duly to the ward attendants to be mailed from Asylum Station, addressed in care of *the Sea*. Had any doctor asked, she would have admitted freely that she had no expectation of reply, only the hope that her vitriol would sink into the waters, not to dissolve and be lost, but to linger and stain, like poisonous Circe. She spat onto some of the pages, bled furtively into others. She dreamed of great reefs and shoals and kelp forests streaming gold in a glissando of pearl-green and knew she had failed. Even now, she could close her eyes and feel the drum and tumble of surf in her blood. It did not seem to point Ezra-ward, only toward the shore of her body, out to the endless, indifferent sea.

The thought tasted like old iron, rusting in bitter spray. "It can't have," Elizabeth said quietly. "There was no one for it to turn to."

"Oh, Lizzie, don't I know it? When you were—when our son—" Ezra was silent, looking down at his dice with their cracked coral faces; he rolled them once on the trim white counterpane, ivory-dotted in twos and threes. "There are tides," he said at last, and looked back at her.

Not far down the hall, the radiator-hissing, clock-ticking stillness of the ward broke with a muted cry and quick footsteps; the gaslight fluttered in its mantle and she was aware that her hands resting on the covers were cold, though her pulse still raced like a riptide. She did not like to think of loose limbs hanging in the glacial dark, turning in icy currents; she did not want to imagine the pattern of gyres and streams, a lyke-road of terrible waters, that could bear a dead man from the mouth of the Arctic Ocean to the mid-Atlantic shore. Ezra was a living man where the warm light touched him, all his scars and flaws and beauties as exact as Elizabeth had not known she remembered them, and then in the colder edging of the moon she saw again the barnacle crust like a fouled hull, the rotten cloth riddled with sponge and anemone. Beneath the hospital scents of carbolic and gardenias, the room smelled of harbor mud and shoreline juniper, the oily smother of the try-works, the brine-swept wild air of the open sea, as though a wind from nowhere tacked about and about the sea-routes that had compassed her dreams and his death. Blue as a boat's painted eyes, his drowned eyes gave her no clues.

She stirred against the pillows, all the small aches and stiffnesses of a woman fifty-nine years old, never graceful and no longer slender, woken in the middle of the night. "You left me worse than a widow, Ezra. The wife of a ghost. A—" She stopped herself with an effort as strong as shouting. *A prisoner,* she had almost said, *a madwoman,* but she had been mad already in her sand-scoured house in New Bedford, mad as any sailor's wife left railing from the shore at the sea that had stolen, one way or another, her man. She had smashed the melon-colored shells and the willow-blue china before her parents' eyes, swept the cabinet cards to the floor and flung down with a clatter the painted panel where a three-masted bark black and white as a petrel had sailed stiffly and precisely over pastel-green waves; she remembered her hands bleeding from slivers of broken window, a kittiwake with trapped wings frantically beating to be free. Afterward she had known the missed opportunity had been not burning the house itself: there was salt in the bones of it now. It would never be anyone's home but the sea's. "The mother of nothing," she said instead, and watched Ezra shift but keep silent. "Or did you think the tides would bring you that back, too?"

"No, Lizzie. I didn't think that."

"Then *what?*"

"You, Elizabeth. Just you. As long as I might. As soon as there was a way. I had to see you." With his glance cast up half in shadow, she could not tell if the faintest edge of a smile moved at his mouth or merely a trickle of salt water. She heard the sea-swallowed words as if she saw them laid out again before her with clay-cold hands: "You've the steadiest eye I know."

In their silence she heard her own breath like an unsteady swell. Crouched intently forward in her rocking chair, the *Galatea's* fourth boatsteerer was watching her with the steadiness she remembered by candlelight, the years when she had told them both into the old stories of her father's library and never imagined herself waiting longer than Penelope, for a husband who was not after all the god in monster's guising but the slip of a soul lost to the underworld, dreaming under the Styx's black water of sleep. Every movement she made, he tracked like a man attentive to the movement of his blood—no, she thought, a tide to the pull of its moon. She wondered if a satellite had ever disowned its ocean, if the great weight and restlessness of waters rejected would go slack. Experimentally, she felt in her own blood, not for direction this time but gravity. Whatever else Ezra McKay had been in life, once she had not thought him a liar.

He moved before she could speak, rummaging through his pockets as suddenly as if he had mislaid pipe or papers, not meeting her gaze now like any ordinarily embarrassed man. She watched him set out the rough fist of ambergris on the bed between them, then a square-rigged ship soot-inked into a polished tooth, then a seal of black soapstone, lounging as if hauled out on its sleekly plump side; she had not touched a piano in almost forty years and she felt, over or under the quick run of notes, the quarter-tone of something discordant, important, unsaid. Slowly, she said, "Are there stars where you are, then, Ezra?" He did not answer; he was still searching as if he could not hear her, bringing out things now that she could not imagine he had carried in his coat or his canvas trousers across any ocean but the last and least known. Here was a handful of pearls dripping with salt-black mud, there a round-bellied bottle streaked green as the plunge of a wave. Silver dollars jumbled with sand dollars, brown-inked logbook pages interleaved with dark plates of baleen. Whale stamps, stick charts, looped strands of pink jade, she felt their weight compressing the mattress springs, opening wrinkles of shadow in the tile-white sheets like leads in sea ice, and when she repeated, "Ezra," he shook his head angrily and something small and goat-eyed and whorled in mother-of-pearl moved its glimmering arms in the palm of his hand. The question was rising in her thoughts like the whale's black back, shouldering ocean and all else aside. She knew before she spoke that it was not the question of a woman in mind of her immortal soul.

"Will there be a ship, Ezra? Will there be a ship for *me*?"

His hands were still full of Bible leaves and holystone, an iceberg's blue-amber shimmer beneath flaring sun dogs; then he put them down on the reef or the pack or the foam of the bed as carefully as if he released a live thing to the waves. Full in the gaslight, his face was as young as she could scarcely imagine either of them being, except that she had been younger still when she had lain with a drowned man in a house of salt and his heart had run to her on its tide. She smelled again snow and ether, fish guts and rotted weed. Vieira's breath had been sweet-sour of a winter morning when she lay as close as she had never dreamed him, one hand against the warm brown grit of his cheek. Her face was cradled in a bright spill of hair, like a beach with the dawn rolling up it, on a clean-ironed pillow that breathed of Castile soap and drying sweat. Under the limitless blue of the ice, her mouth filled with salt, and then her lungs, and then her bones. She knew him then, the sea and the sailor, the face and the mask. "Lizzie," he said gently in his voice of deep waters, "I'll wait."

Clear as the sight of a sextant, she watched him rattle the coral dice between cupped hands, slick and limpet-studded, scarred and brown as rope; she saw the throw and his shy, startled, stranger's grin, leaping to meet the danger he had always known she was. His name in her mouth was a seabird's cry, "Ezra—" She finished it to the moonlight and gaslight, hissing faintly in the creak of the wind. The chair rocked a little, as if its occupant had stood abruptly. Neither mussel shells nor kelp nor cutting spades lay in her bed. Her hands were freezing cold.

A sane woman might have been screaming, Elizabeth thought, but she would never be sane again and she had screamed enough. Stiff in the shoulders, she put her hands beneath the covers and did not imagine that she could feel the small worn corners of coral or the sheeting ice of a glacier; when she had almost stopped shivering, she turned down the gaslight until it was too blue and tiny to disturb the white froth of the moon. "Ezra," she said aloud, knowing he would not hear her, not knowing if the sea might, rushing along the inside of her veins in sinkings and upwellings, not to be halted until, like the song, it ran dry. The night nurse's footsteps paused at her door and passed on. In the bright and war-wracked autumn of 1918, Elizabeth McKay tasted salt on her lips that she could not remember crying, spray from a shore she had not seen since the last century. "Ezra," she said again, "I'll hold you to that," and turned to her bed to see if she would wake in the morning or merely leave pearls behind.

53

I have attempted here to lay bare with the unreserve of a last hour's confession the terms of my relation with the sea, which beginning mysteriously, like any great passion the inscrutable Gods send to mortals, went on unreasoning and invincible, surviving the test of disillusion, defying the disenchantment that lurks in every day of a strenuous life; went on full of love's delight and love's anguish, facing them in open-eyed exultation, without bitterness and without repining, from the first hour to the last.

—Joseph Conrad, *The Mirror of the Sea* (1906)

Acknowledgements

For the words collected here, my thanks to John Benson, Jeannelle M. Ferreira, Gemma Files, Michael Fiveash, Lila Garrott-Wejksnora, Greer Gilman, Alfred and Bernice Madinek Glixman, Mitchell Hart, Niels-Viggo Hobbs, Caitlín R. Kiernan, Layla Lawlor, R.B. Lemberg, Hestia Hermia Linsky-Noyes, Elise Matthesen, Leonard C. Muellner, Shweta Narayan, Rob Noyes, Matthew Revert, Ishita Singh, Shoshana Stern, Romie Stott, Marika and Jaime Taaffe, Tybalt Autolycus Taaffe, Anna Tambour, Lynne M. Thomas, Michael Damian Thomas, and Luis Yglesias. To the music of Peter Bellamy, Desperate Journalist, Felled, the Klezmatics, Moss of Moonlight, the Watersons, Yehudi Wyner, the Young Tradition, and more chanteys than there are seas. To the films of Gore Verbinski and John Ford. To the North Atlantic.

Publication Credits

"Dive" copyright © 2017, first appeared in *Not One of Us #58*. "The Coast Guard" copyright © 2009, first appeared in in *Sirenia Digest #41*. "The Parable of the Albatross" copyright © 2016, first appeared in in *Stone Telling #13: Hope*. "Firebrands" copyright © 2015, first appeared in *Through the Gate #7*. "Capta" copyright © 2020, first appeared in in *Past Tense* (ed. John Benson). "Colonial" copyright © 2021, first appeared in in *Mithila Review #15*. "He Should Marry the Daughter of the Angel of Death" copyright © 2020, first appeared in *Strange Horizons 31 August 2020*. "qe-ra-si-ja" copyright © 2022, original to this collection. "Σειρήνοιϊν" copyright © 2015, first appeared in *Uncanny Magazine #5*. "The Secret Language of Water" copyright © 2020, first appeared in *Not One of Us #63*. "As the Tide Came Flowing In" copyright © 2022, original to this collection.

About the Author

Sonya Taaffe reads dead languages, tells living stories, and loves the spaces in between. Her Lambda-nominated, Rhysling-winning short fiction and poetry have been previously collected in *Forget the Sleepless Shores*, *Ghost Signs*, *A Mayse-Bikhl*, *Postcards from the Province of Hyphens*, and *Singing Innocence and Experience*. She lives with one of her husbands and both of her cats in Somerville, Massachusetts where she writes about film and remains proud of naming a Kuiper belt object.